T0100861

To

.....

From

.....

Date

.....

ColoringFAITH
Jesus Calling®
Adult Coloring Book
Creative Coloring & Hand Lettering
Sarah Young
Experience Peace in His Presence
Thomas Nelson
Since 1798

Jesus Calling® Creative Coloring and Hand Lettering Book

Copyright © 2017 by Sarah Young

All quotes from *Jesus Calling®*.

All rights reserved. No portion of this book may be reproduced, stored in a retrieval system, or transmitted in any form or by any means—electronic, mechanical, photocopy, recording, scanning, or other—except for brief quotations in critical reviews or articles, without the prior written permission of the publisher.

Published in Nashville, Tennessee, by Thomas Nelson. Thomas Nelson is a registered trademark of HarperCollins Christian Publishing, Inc.

Unless otherwise noted, Scripture quotations are taken from the Holy Bible, New International Version®, NIV®. Copyright © 1973, 1978, 1984 by Biblica, Inc.® Used by permission of Zondervan. All rights reserved worldwide. www.zondervan.com. The "NIV" and "New International Version" are trademarks registered in the United States Patent and Trademark Office by Biblica, Inc.®

Other Scripture quotations are from the following sources: New King James Version®. © 1982 by Thomas Nelson. Used by permission. All rights reserved.

ISBN 978-0-7180-9126-2

Printed in China

21 22 23 24 25 /DSC/ 23 22 21 20 19 18 17 16 15

Introduction

Hand lettering is for everyone!

Hand lettering is one of the biggest trends out there. What's so fun about art—even hand lettering—is that the sky is the limit. Whether you've had formal training or just want to try your hand and have fun with it, hand lettering is for any skill level. With a few basic principles, time, and practice, you can develop your own unique style and try new and creative techniques each day.

There are so many types of lettering tools on the market that it can be a bit overwhelming. A small investment in a few tools will take you far! You can create gorgeous hand-lettered pieces with pencils, fine felt-tip markers, brush pens, watercolor brushes, and more.

In this book, in addition to gorgeous, intricate illustrations to color, you will find hand-lettering designs of quotes taken from the Bible and from Sarah Young's 365-day devotional *Jesus Calling*®. You can trace these designs with an ultra-fine marker or color them in with a paintbrush or brush pen. You'll also see that some of the words are shaded gray, which will help guide you through each stroke.

As you begin this creative journey, remember that it doesn't have to be complicated. Enjoy the practice of hand lettering as you reflect on Scripture and trace quotes that remind you of God's unending love for you. For additional help, there are lined practice pages with sample letters in the back of the book. Grab a pencil and a sheet of paper or a practice sketch pad. Trace over the sample letters or copy them side by side on your paper. You can thicken downstrokes (the lines that occur anytime you draw downward when you create letters) or you can color in downstrokes (or weight your downstrokes heavily with a brush or brush pen). Include details and swirls among the words and letters for added artistry.

Basic Principles

A few basic principles will guide your hand lettering throughout this book:

- Sketch out your ideas
- Trace and fill in
- Add details
- Mix and match fonts
- Have fun!

About This Book

This one-of-a-kind adult coloring and hand-lettering book contains more than 100 illustrations to color and hand-lettering quotes to trace. This book offers you a time to relax and think about God's Word while you create beautiful pieces of art. Quotes from the #1 bestseller *Jesus Calling*® fill these pages with themes of thankfulness and trust in the Lord and the Peace only Jesus can bring. These themes are quite prevalent in the Bible and are a vital part of a close relationship with the Lord. Experience a deeper relationship with Jesus as you focus on His words of hope, guidance, and peace.

I am far more

REAL than

the world you can

see, hear,

and touch.

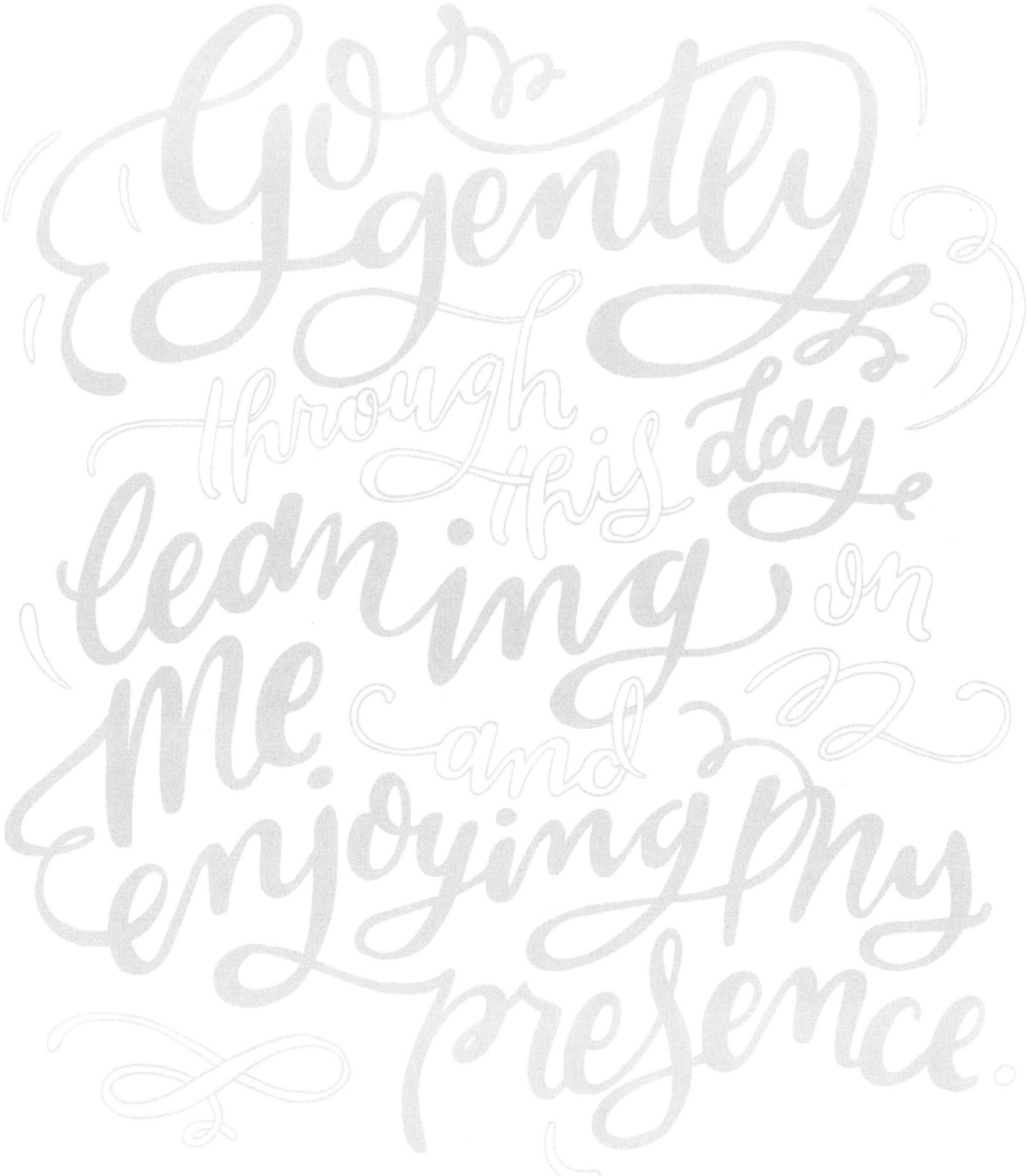
Go gently
through this day
leaning on
me and
enjoying my
presence.

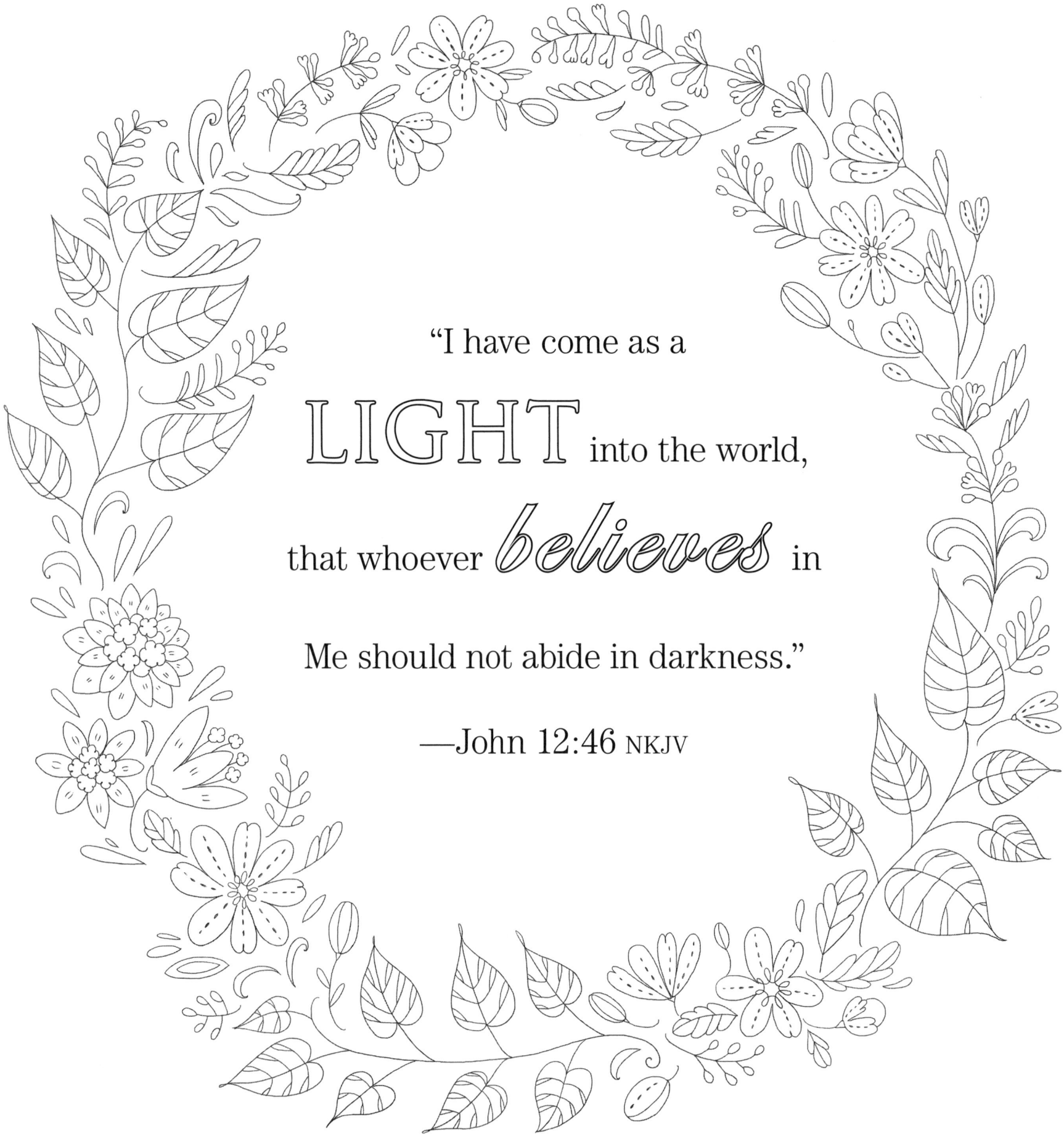

"I have come as a

LIGHT into the world,

that whoever *believes* in

Me should not abide in darkness."

—John 12:46 NKJV

I CARE AS MUCH
ABOUT YOUR
tiny
trust
STEPS
THROUGH DAILY LIFE
AS ABOUT YOUR
DRAMATIC
leaps
OF
faith

You need

not fear the

future,

for I am already

THERE.

We have
this hope
as an
ANCHOR
for the soul,
firm &
secure.
Hebrews 6:19

Trust and

thankfulness

will get you safely

through this day. Trust

PROTECTS

you from worrying and obsessing.

Thankfulness KEEPS you

from criticizing and complaining.

I am
WITH
YOU
& for you.
YOU FACE
nothing
alone—
NOTHING!

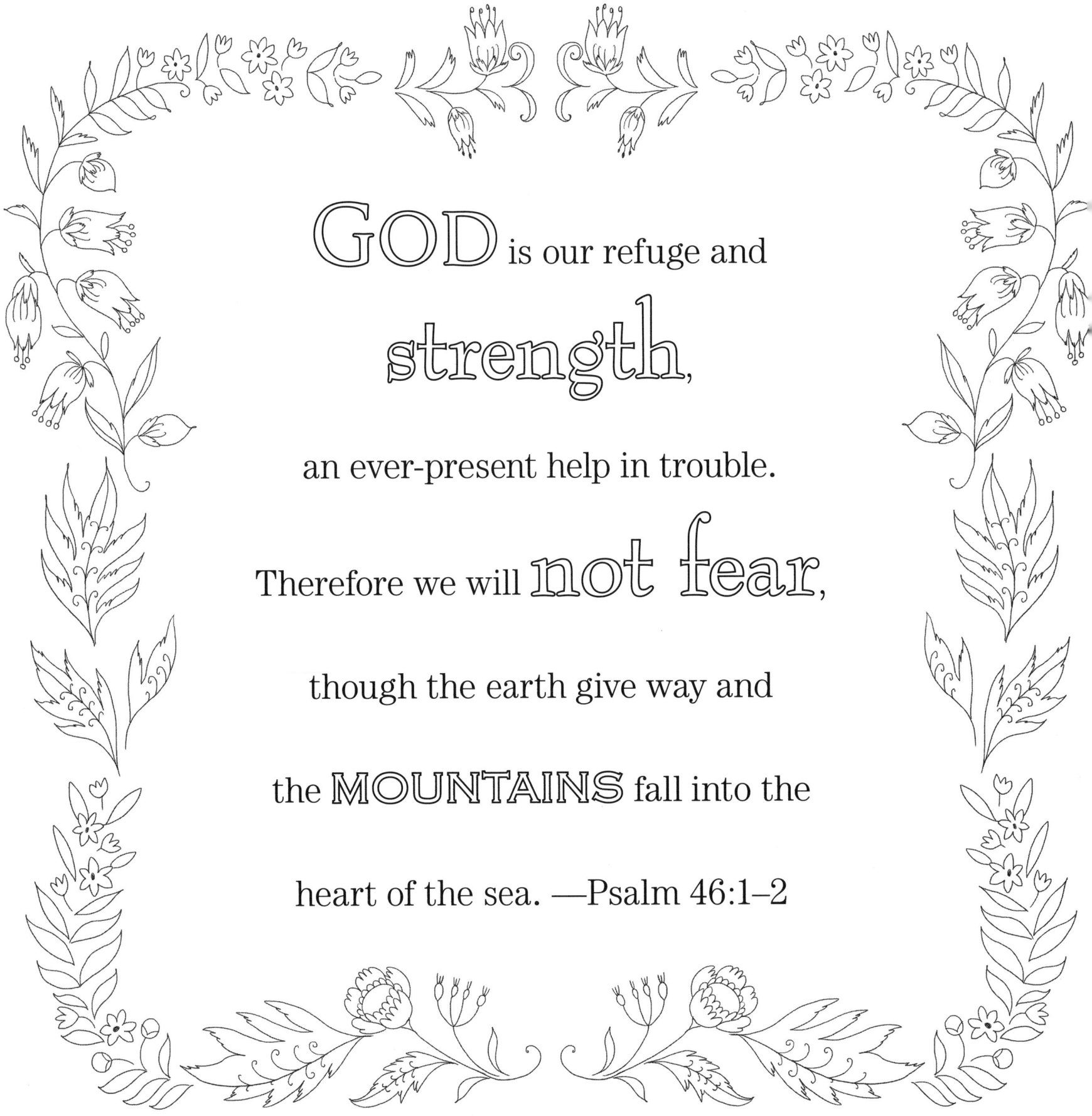
GOD is our refuge and
strength,
an ever-present help in trouble.
Therefore we will not fear,
though the earth give way and
the MOUNTAINS fall into the
heart of the sea. —Psalm 46:1–2

whenever you find yourself
WORRYING
about the future,
repent
AND
return to ME.

I am *training*

you to hold in your

heart a dual focus:

My continual Presence

and the **hope**

of **HEAVEN**.

TRUST is a Golden PATHWAY to HEAVEN. WHEN YOU WALK on this path, YOU live above YOUR circumstances.

Entrust your loved ones

to Me; release them into

My **protective** care.

They are much safer with Me than

in your clinging hands.

Look to the Lord and his strength; seek his face always.
1 Chronicles 16:11

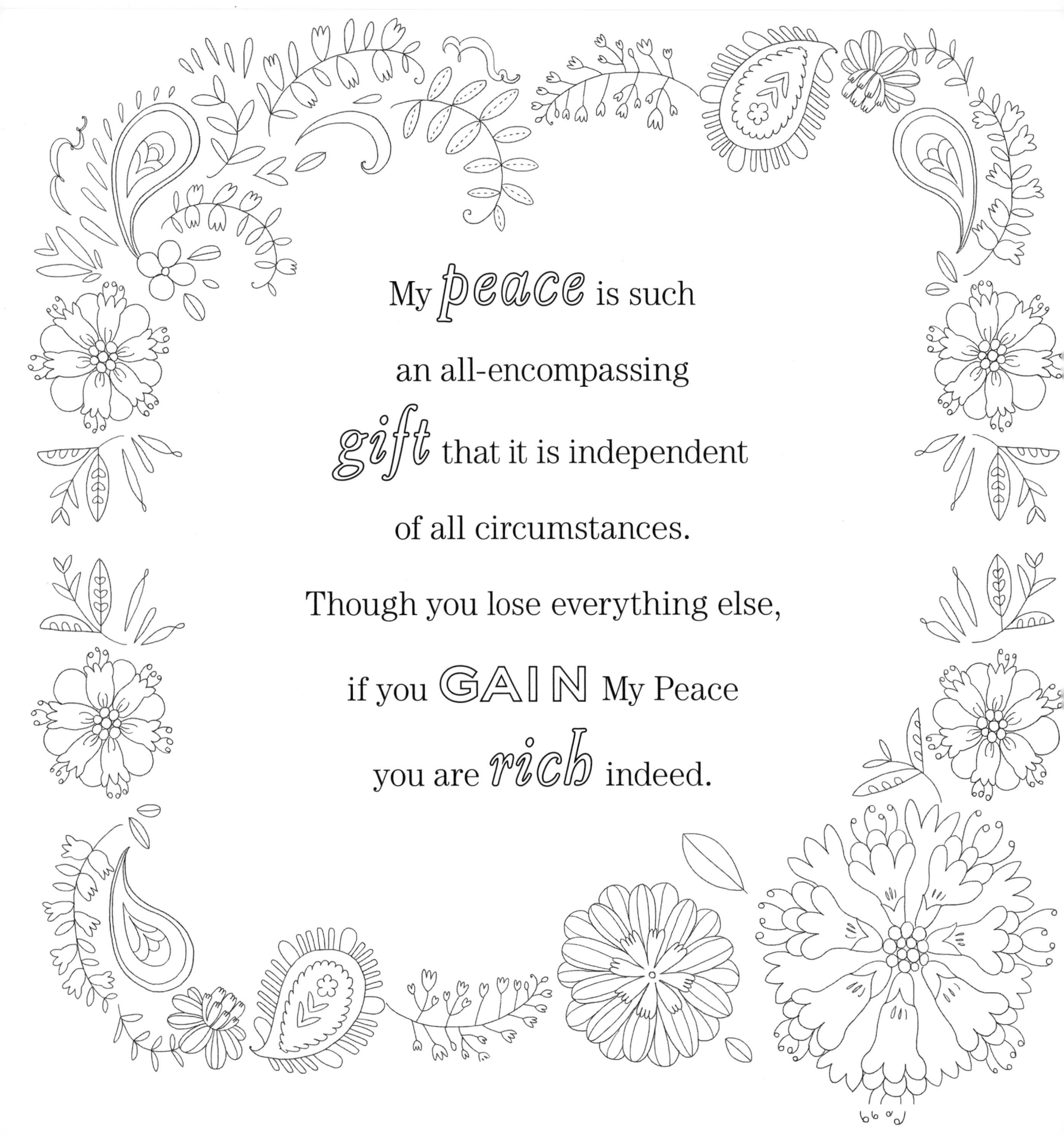

My *peace* is such

an all-encompassing

gift that it is independent

of all circumstances.

Though you lose everything else,

if you GAIN My Peace

you are *rich* indeed.

I,
the Lover of
your Soul,
understand you
perfectly
AND
LOVE · YOU
ETERNALLY.

The way to WALK

through demanding days

is to GRIP My hand

tightly and stay in close

communication with Me.

MY
kingdom
IS NOT ABOUT
EARNING AND DESERVING
IT IS ABOUT
believing
AND
receiving

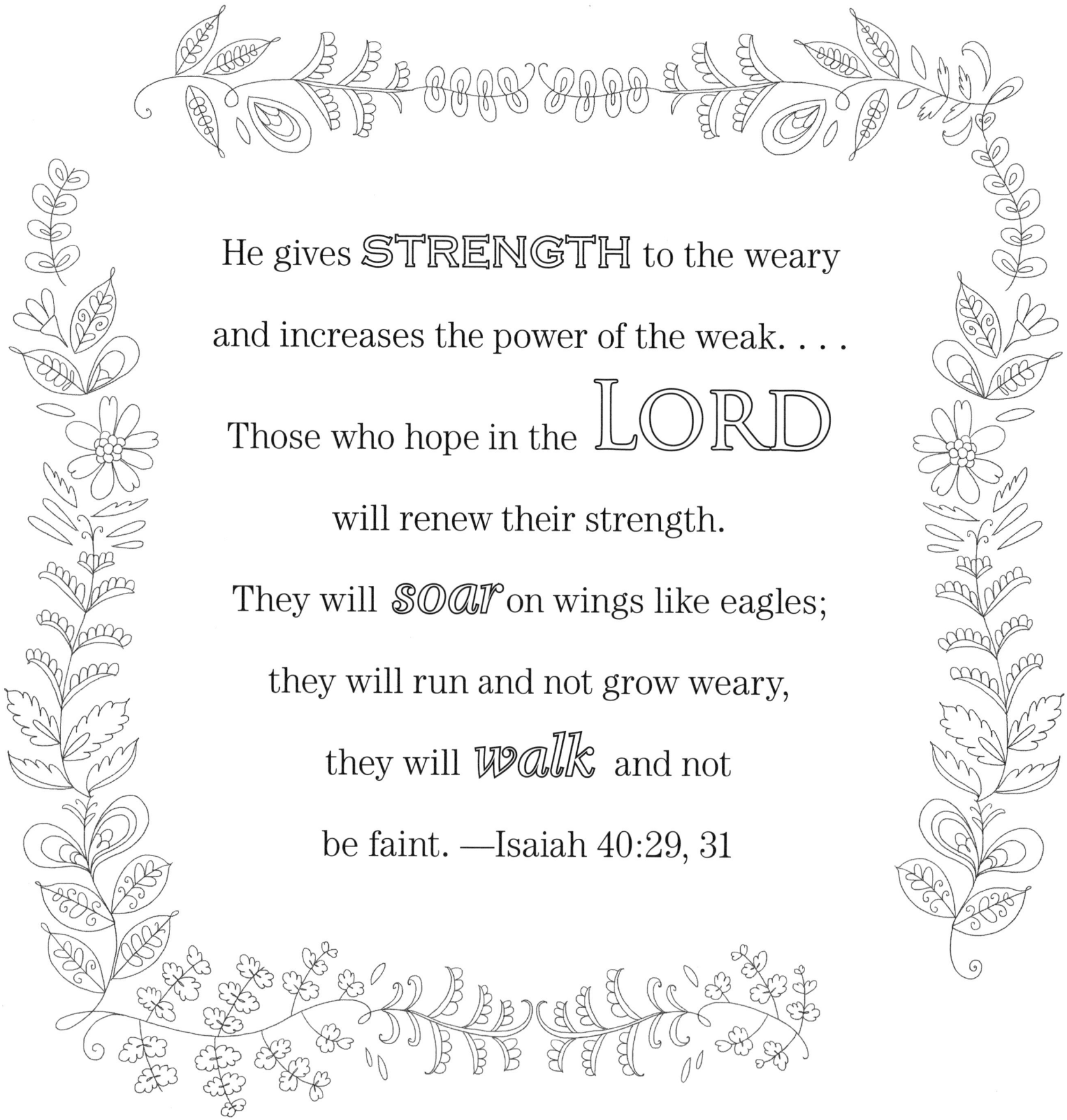

He gives STRENGTH to the weary

and increases the power of the weak. . . .

Those who hope in the LORD

will renew their strength.

They will *soar* on wings like eagles;

they will run and not grow weary,

they will *walk* and not

be faint. —Isaiah 40:29, 31

I am nearer than you dare believe, closer than the air you breathe.

I know

every

step of the

journey

ahead of you,

all the way to

heaven.

EACH MOMENT
YOU CAN CHOOSE
TO PRACTICE

My Presence

OR TO PRACTICE THE
PRESENCE OF PROBLEMS

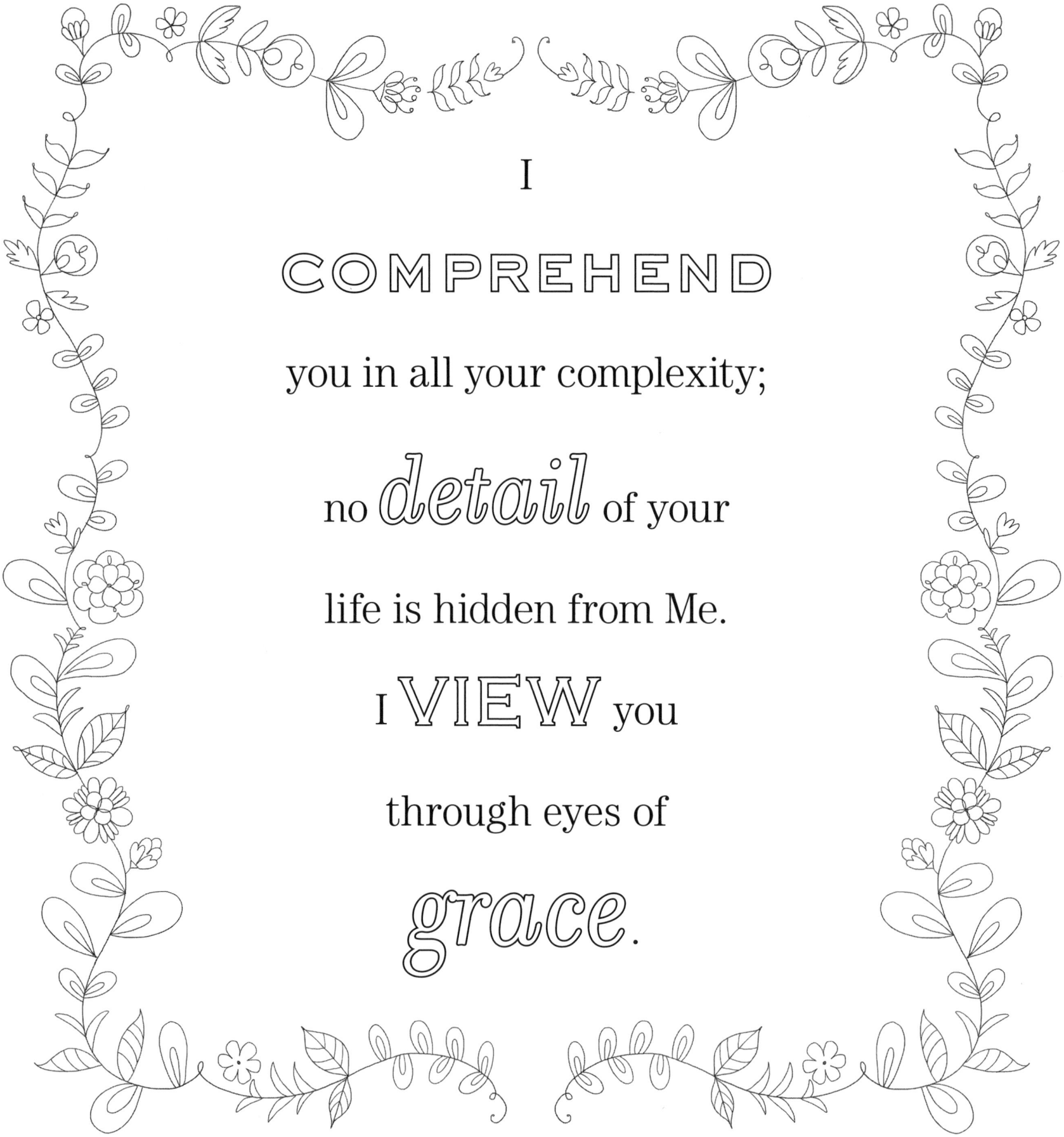

I

COMPREHEND

you in all your complexity;

no *detail* of your

life is hidden from Me.

I VIEW you

through eyes of

grace.

I will praise you,
O Lord my God,
with all my
heart.
Psalm 86:12
NKJV

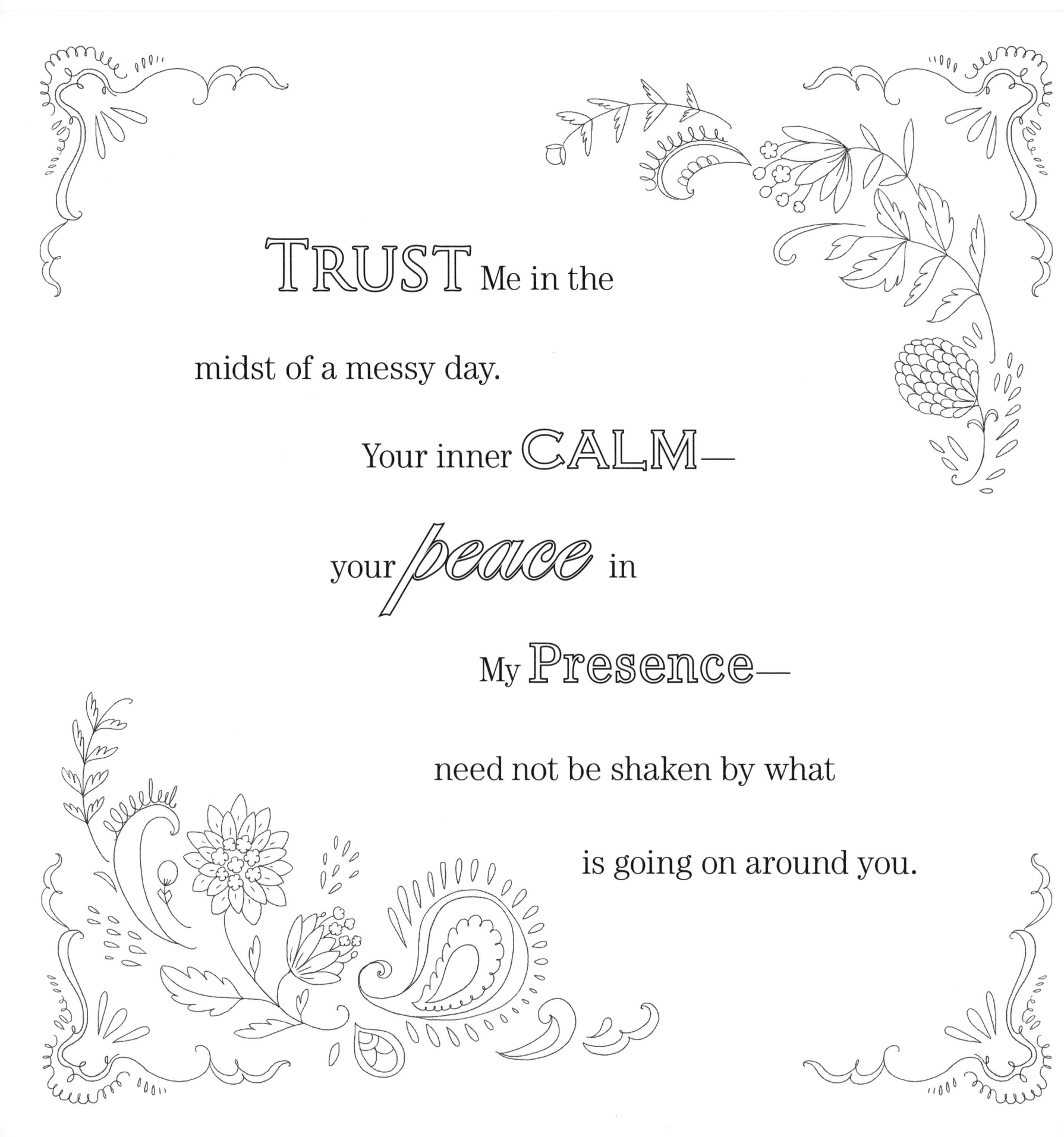

TRUST Me in the

midst of a messy day.

Your inner CALM—

your *peace* in

My Presence—

need not be shaken by what

is going on around you.

HOPE
is a
golden
cord
connecting you to
HEAVEN.

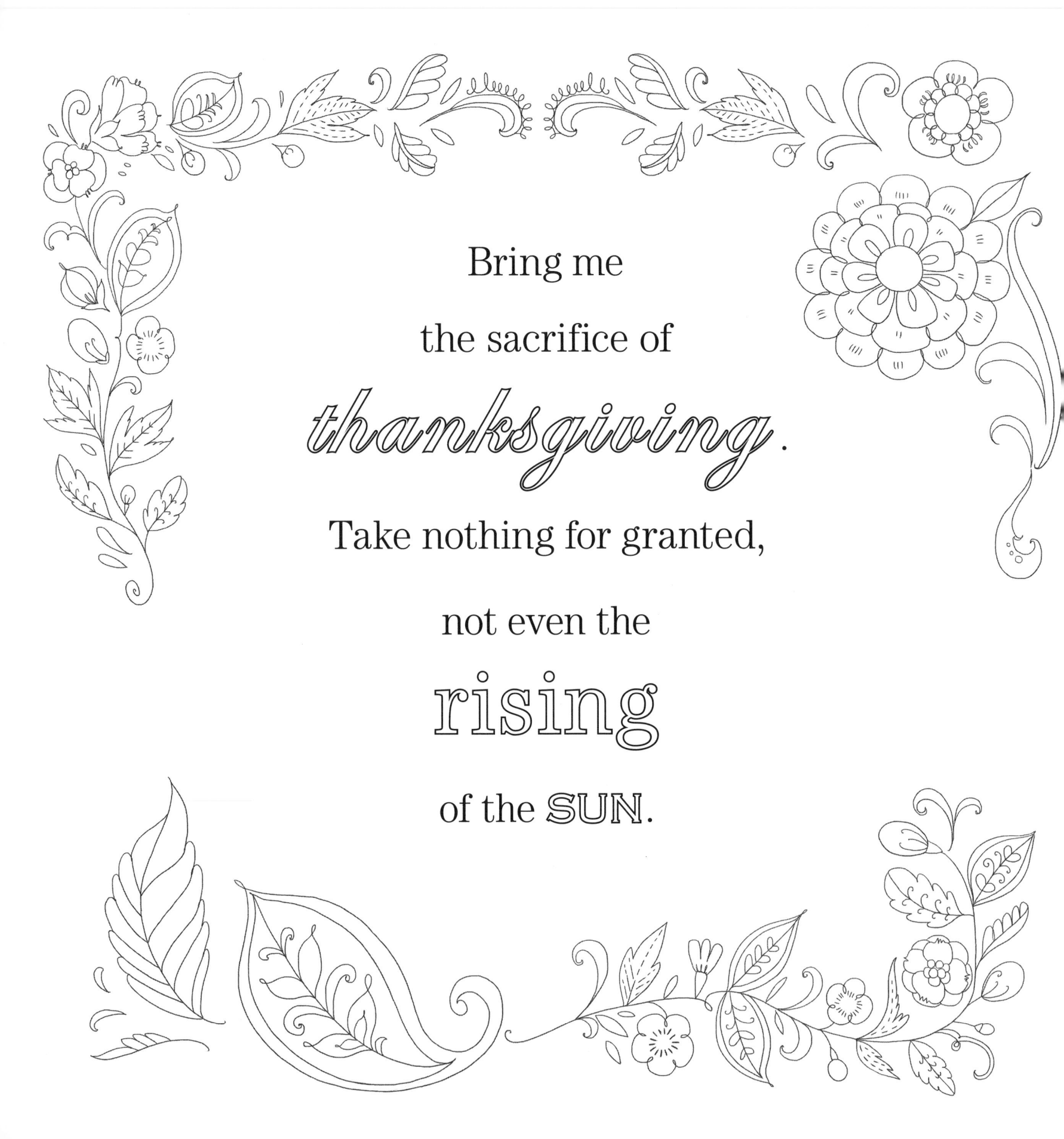

Bring me

the sacrifice of

thanksgiving.

Take nothing for granted,

not even the

rising

of the SUN.

NOTHING
YOU DO OR
DON'T DO
CAN SEPARATE
YOU FROM MY
love.

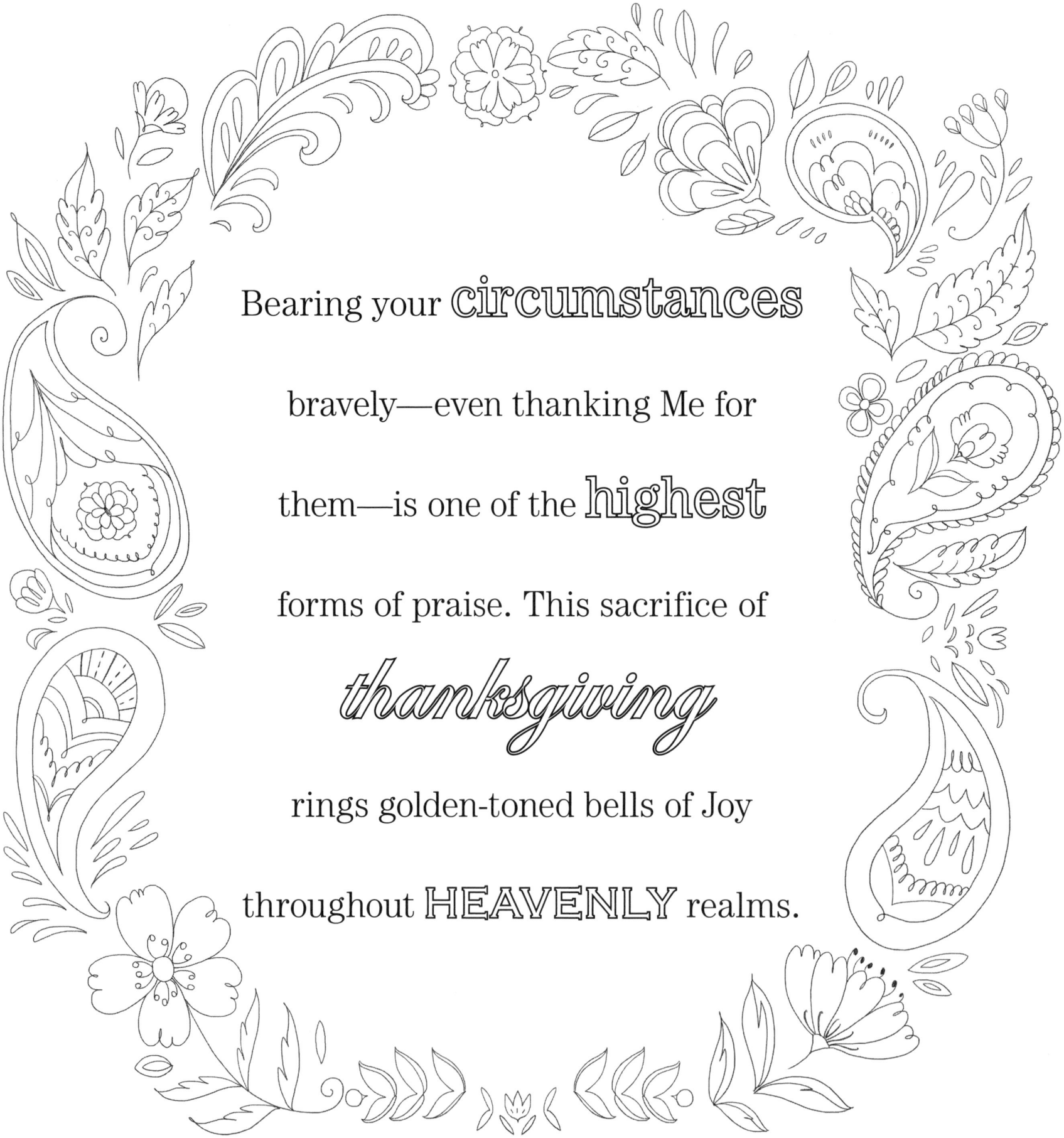

Bearing your **circumstances**

bravely—even thanking Me for

them—is one of the **highest**

forms of praise. This sacrifice of

thanksgiving

rings golden-toned bells of Joy

throughout **HEAVENLY** realms.

You are my lamp, O Lord; the Lord turns my darkness into light.
2 Samuel 22:29

Pray about
EVERYTHING;
then, leave
OUTCOMES
up to Me.

Receive My Peace
AS YOU LIE DOWN TO
"Sleep"
WITH
thankful thoughts
PLAYING A lullaby IN YOUR mind.

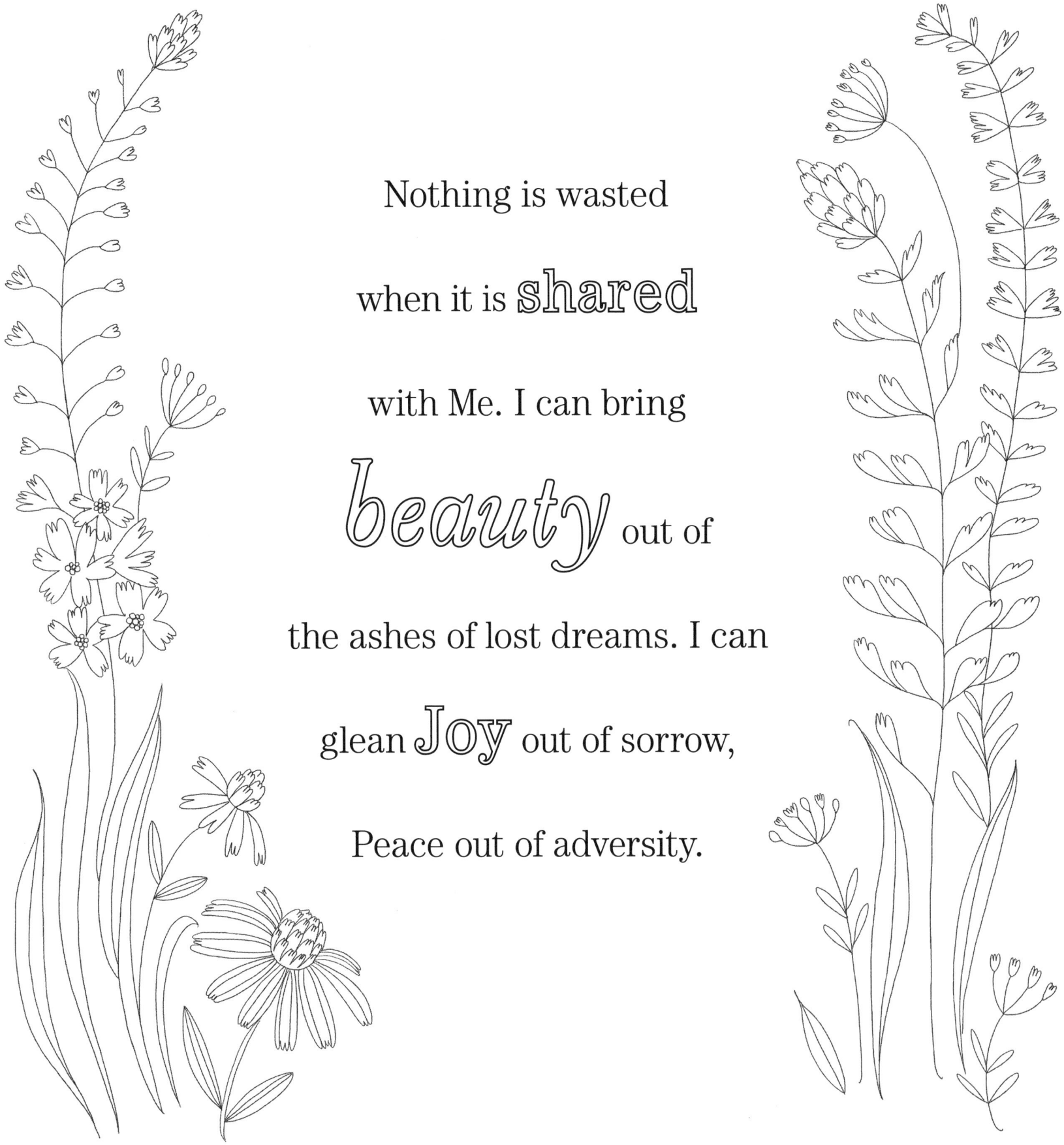

Nothing is wasted

when it is **shared**

with Me. I can bring

beauty out of

the ashes of lost dreams. I can

glean **Joy** out of sorrow,

Peace out of adversity.

Come to Me.
Come to Me.
Come to Me.

This is My continual invitation to you, proclaimed in

holy whispers.

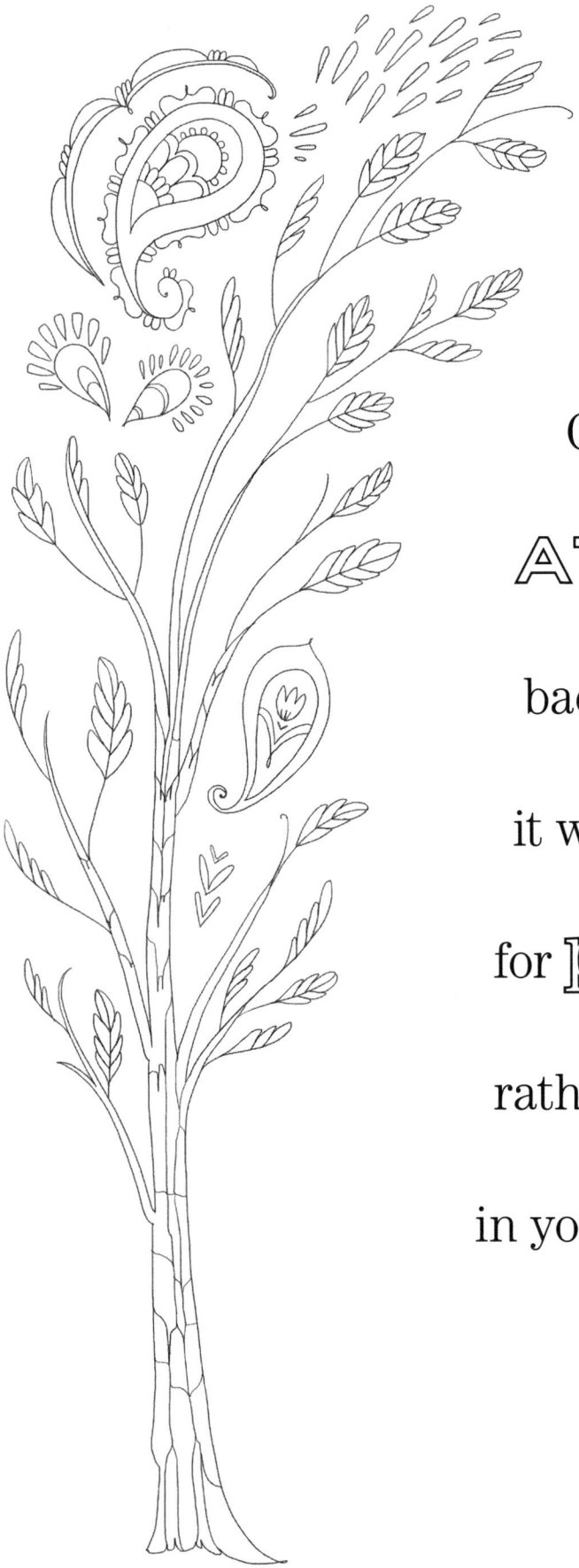

Gently bring your

ATTENTION

back to Me, whenever

it wanders away. I look

for persistence—

rather than perfection—

in your WALK with Me.

O God,
YOU ARE
MY
God,
EARNESTLY
I seek
you
Psalm 63:1

Every time you thank Me,

you **acknowledge** that I am

your **LORD** and **PROVIDER**.

This is the proper stance for a child of

God: **receiving with thanksgiving**.

Take a DEEP breath
AND Dive INTO THE depths OF
ABSOLUTE Trust IN me.

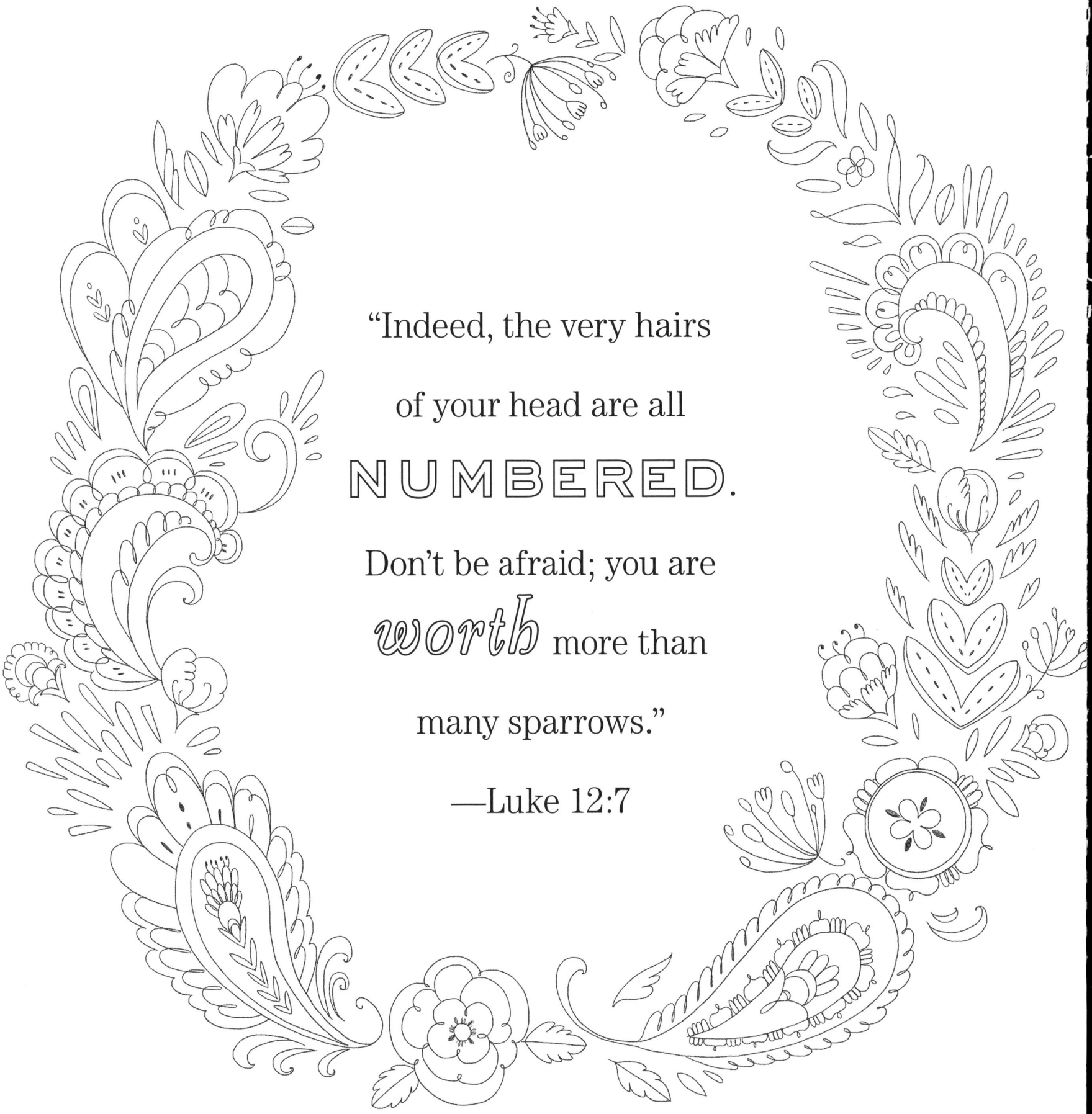

"Indeed, the very hairs

of your head are all

NUMBERED.

Don't be afraid; you are

worth more than

many sparrows."

—Luke 12:7

marvel at the beauty of a life intertwined with my presence.

When you walk through

a day with childlike delight,

savoring every blessing,

you proclaim your trust in Me,

your ever-present SHEPHERD.

Your inner calm—
YOUR
peace
IN
my presence—
need not be
shaken
by what is going on
AROUND YOU.

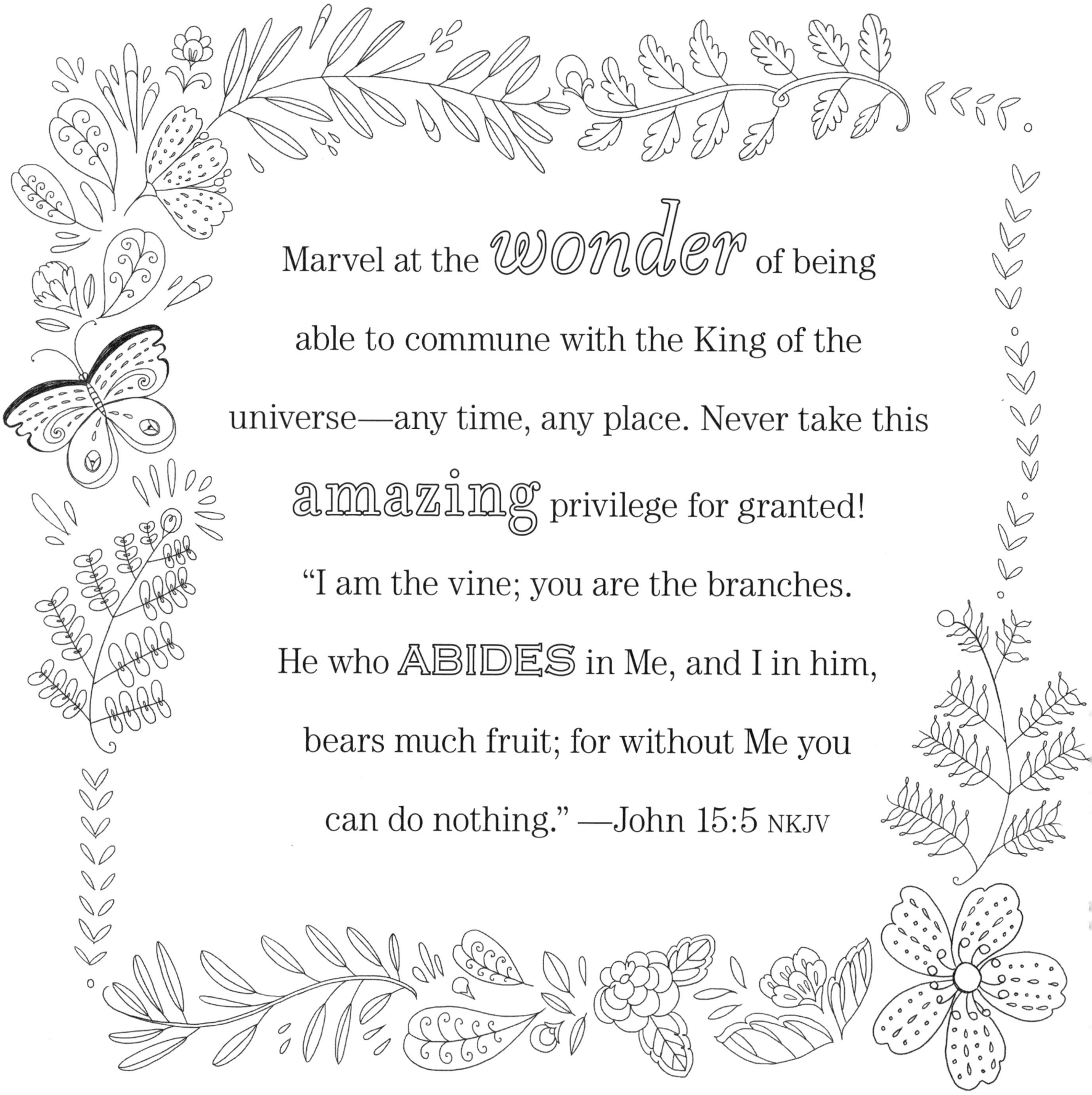

Marvel at the **wonder** of being able to commune with the King of the universe—any time, any place. Never take this **amazing** privilege for granted!

"I am the vine; you are the branches. He who **ABIDES** in Me, and I in him, bears much fruit; for without Me you can do nothing." —John 15:5 NKJV

Rather than
planning &
evaluating
practice
trusting
& thanking
Me continually.

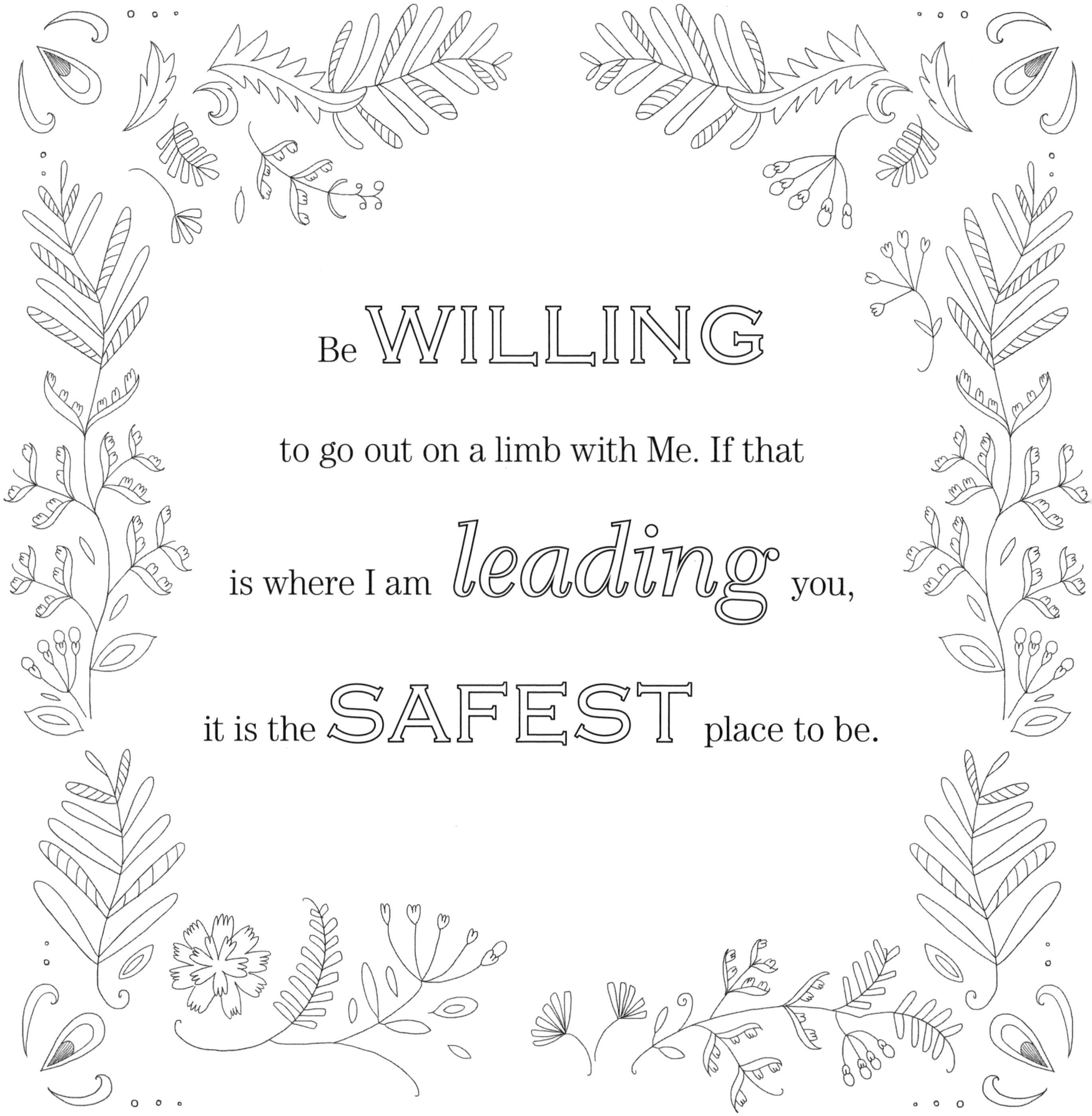
Be WILLING
to go out on a limb with Me. If that
is where I am leading you,
it is the SAFEST place to be.

I will lie down
&
sleep
in
peace,
for you alone,
O Lord,
make me dwell
in safety.
Psalm 4:8

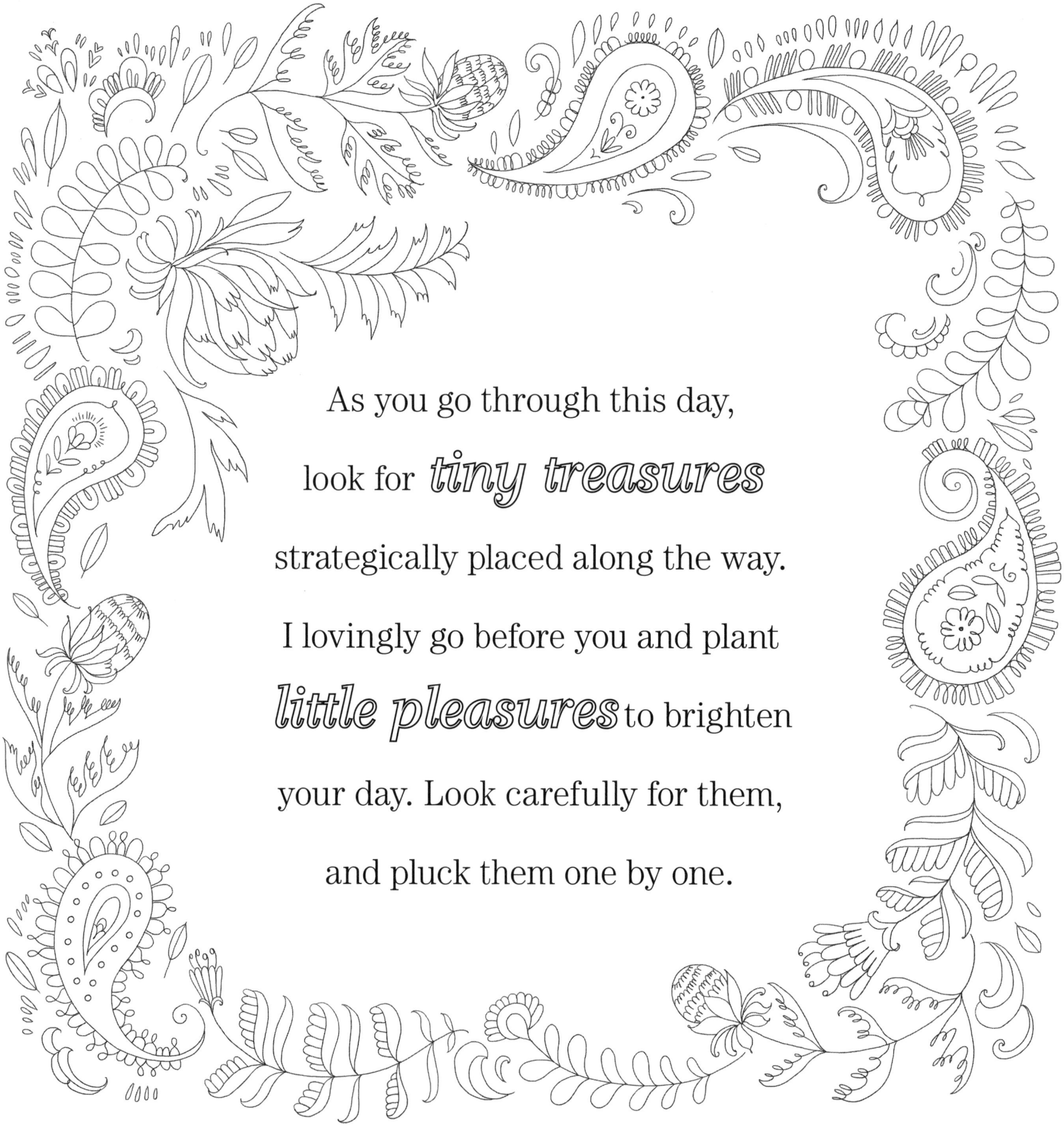

As you go through this day,

look for **tiny treasures**

strategically placed along the way.

I lovingly go before you and plant

little pleasures to brighten

your day. Look carefully for them,

and pluck them one by one.

Walk with Me in holy Trust

But I am like an olive tree

flourishing

in the house of God; I trust

in God's unfailing LOVE for

ever and ever. —Psalm 52:8

HEAR ME
SAYING,
"Peace,
be still!"
to YOUR
restless
HEART.

Practice TRUSTING Me

during quiet days, when nothing

much seems to be happening.

Then when storms come,

your trust BALANCE will be

sufficient to see you through.

Practice Pages